MICHAEL HARDCASTLE

United!

Bank Vale United badly need to win if they
are to have any chance of the Championship!
Then Kevin Ripley has the brilliant idea of
buying a player from another team. But
although Nick Abel-Smith may be a good scorer,
he's also a troublemaker and Gary and Keith
have their work cut out to keep Bank Vale United
together.

An exciting sequel to In the Net

MICHAEL HARDCASTLE

United!

Illustrated by Trevor Stubley

A Magnet Book

Also by Michael Hardcastle in Magnet Books

IN THE NET
FREE KICK
AWAY FROM HOME
SOCCER SPECIAL
HALF A TEAM
THE SATURDAY HORSE
THE SWITCH HORSE
ROAR TO VICTORY
FAST FROM THE GATE

First published in Great Britain 1973
by Methuen Children's Books Ltd
11 New Fetter Lane, London EC4P 4EE
This paperback edition published 1974
Reprinted 1977, 1982 and 1985
Text copyright © 1973 by Michael Hardcastle
Illustrations copyright © 1973
by Trevor Stubley
Printed in Great Britain by
Richard Clay (The Chaucer Press) Ltd, Bungay, Suffolk
ISBN 0 416 79840 3

One

Kevin Ripley almost beat his fists on the ground in anger as the United defence let in another goal. Twice Kevin himself had given United the lead— and twice he had seen it wiped out because of mistakes at the other end.

Before the start of the match with Raw Nook Rovers in the Sunday Junior League he had been confident United would win easily. 'We'll pulverize this lot,' he had told Keith Nash, United's captain. Pulverize was his favourite word these days. 'We'll absolutely slaughter them. They're not in the same class as us.'

Bank Vale United were in need of a good win. This was their fourth match of the new season in the League. So far they had lost two games and drawn one.

'We've got no chance of the Championship if

we don't start winning soon,' Keith had told the team in his pre-match tactical talk. He took his responsibilities as captain very seriously. He played as a half-back and was a good defender. Kevin, the star of the forward line, wished that the rest of the defence was as skilful. Raw Nook had scored both their goals as a result of feeble tackling by United's full-backs.

'There's only one thing for it,' Kevin said to Harvey Slater as they lined up again in the centre circle. 'We'll just have to score a whole bag of goals.

'Then if our defence keep giving 'em away we'll have a few in reserve. I don't care if we win 10-9 as long as we win.'

Harvey, United's tall, long-haired centre-forward, just nodded. He himself hadn't managed to get the ball into the net once this season. He suspected that Kevin was getting at him for failing so often to score. Harvey thought deeply about his game but he didn't know why he was having such a bad time.

As soon as he received the ball from his centre-forward, Kevin set off up the field as if he meant to beat Rovers all on his own. That was something he thought he was capable of doing, anyway. He evaded two tackles cleverly with his body-swerve and headed for the penalty area. Harvey Slater came pounding up in his wake but Kevin just ignored him. When he looked up he saw that Gary Ansell, United's fast and tricky right-winger, was signalling that he wanted the ball.

With his left foot Kevin sent a long pass to the right wing. It was so well placed that George Best would have been pleased with it. Gary took the ball in his stride. A Rovers full-back came at him but Gary neatly pushed the ball past him and then sprinted after it. The full-back was slow to recover. Two other defenders moved out towards Gary and that left a lot of free space in the middle.

Gary tried to lift the ball into the centre for Harvey to try a header. Instead, he sliced the ball. Almost as if he'd expected that to happen, Kevin darted to one side and reached the ball before anyone else. He knew exactly where Harvey Slater was and very firmly he turned the ball back to him.

Harvey had a clear sight of goal. The Rovers goalkeeper made no move to come off his line, so

7

Harvey had a big enough target. When the ball came to him there wasn't an opponent within five yards of him. But, instead of steadying himself and picking his spot, Harvey swung at the ball immediately. And ballooned it over the bar.

Kevin was furious. 'That was an absolute sitter —I gave it you on a plate. You idiot, you should have taken your time,' he yelled at Harvey, who could only mumble an apology.

That let-off seemed to inspire Rovers and for the next few minutes they played some neat, controlled football. Once again United's defence came under pressure. Slater, as if to make up for his blunder in front of goal, dropped back to help them out. His height and weight were useful in stemming the wave of attacks by the Raw Nook boys. At one point he forced his way out of a ruck of players with the ball at his feet and, after a glance up the field, he sent it skimming over the turf to Johnny Butler.

It was a perfect pass to United's little left-winger. Johnny, who could move like a hare, set off up his flank at a tremendous pace. Soon Kevin was screaming for the ball. He wanted to be in the game all the time and he hadn't received a pass for several minutes. Johnny, however, was not ready to pass to anyone yet. His speed alone carried him past a couple of opponents and he was almost at the by-line before he turned inside.

Suddenly he stopped dead. Anxiously he looked round for someone to give the ball to but there was no team-mate at hand. He was on his own.

Kevin now raced across the field towards his winger. Johnny started to move again as an opponent also came at him but he stumbled over the ball—and sat down. The Raw Nook player was probably as surprised by this mishap as Johnny himself but he didn't take his eye off the ball. He reached it just ahead of Kevin and booted it into touch. He'd seen what Kevin could do and he wasn't going to risk a clash with him on the ball.

Taking the throw-in himself, Kevin lobbed the ball at Johnny Butler. The winger still hadn't got over the shock of the way in which he'd lost the ball. He remained completely motionless as the ball hit his knees and rebounded to Kevin. That was all that Kevin wanted.

Pushing the ball ahead of him, swerving briskly

round two opponents and with only one aim in mind Kevin cut into the penalty area. He saw that Gary Ansell was unmarked on the other side of the box but he didn't release the ball. He was going to have a shot—and he was going to complete his hat-trick. He might have done all that— if he hadn't been sent flying by a hefty charge in the back from one of the Rovers full-backs.

Kevin was on his feet in an instant, yelling for a penalty kick. The referee didn't think twice about agreeing with him. Dramatically he blew his whistle in a long blast and pointed to the spot.

'I'll take it, I'll take it,' Kevin insisted as Keith Nash came running up. 'I'd've scored anyway so it's only fair I should take it.'

Keith looked doubtful. He glanced at Gary Ansell, who usually took the penalty kicks awarded to United. Gary was awaiting his captain's instructions and saying nothing. From the ten kicks he'd taken so far he'd scored eight goals and he expected to take this one. On the other hand, he could sympathize with Kevin's feelings about being robbed of his chance of a hat-trick.

'I don't think you're calm enough to take this kick,' Keith told Kevin. True enough, Kevin appeared very agitated. He was also clutching the ball and seemed in no mood to hand it over to anyone else.

'Rubbish!' Kevin shot back at him. 'I'm as calm as you are—and a lot calmer than their goalie. I just want to get on with it. We're wasting valuable time.'

'Okay,' Keith consented. He daren't look at Gary Ansell. 'But for heaven's sake, don't miss it, Kevin.'

The penalty taker made a great fuss about placing the ball precisely on the spot and wiping imaginary mud off his right boot. The Raw Nook goalkeeper looked very nervous indeed although he'd already shown during the match that he was a good player.

Kevin hesitated for several moments to unsettle the goalie still further. Keith feared the referee was going to order Kevin to hurry up. Then, from a long run, Kevin hit the ball hard to the goal-keeper's left. But it was neither hard enough nor wide enough. The goalie jumped to his left and gathered the ball easily at chest height. His team-mates cheered loudly as their hero kicked the ball away to safety.

Kevin was furious with himself but he didn't try to make any excuses. He knew he had hit a bad shot. Now he would have to make up for his lapse. As he ran back to join in the game again he muttered 'sorry' to his captain. Gary Ansell was generous enough to call out: 'Hard lines, Kevin.' At the same time, Gary supposed that when next United were awarded a penalty he would be the player to take the kick.

Raw Nook's confidence flooded back and once more they went on to the attack. They had an inside-left just as good as Kevin Ripley. He was never out of the game for long and when he received a good pass from his centre-half he headed straight for goal. Keith Nash made a sliding tackle that was spectacular—but not successful. The inside-left, Geoff Foley, kept going until another defender went at him full tilt.

Foley switched the ball to his winger, ran into position for a return pass and now was in the United penalty area. Alex Hornsey, Bank Vale's goalie, was jigging up and down on his line. There was now no cover at all in front of him and he was uncertain what to do. He knew that any moment the Raw Nook attacker would have a shot.

Alex had to do something. He rushed out of his goal to fling himself at the ball. Geoff Foley chose his moment well. He flicked the ball forward under the goalkeeper's diving body—and into the net.

Bank Vale United 2, Raw Nook Rovers 3.

A few minutes later the referee signalled the end of the game. United had lost for the third time in only four matches.

As the team trooped off the field no one was in the mood to say very much. Each player had his own thoughts about why they'd lost and what the team's chances of success were in the future. None of them imagined he would be dropped for the next match. They all knew that United had a shortage of players able to turn out regularly on Sunday afternoons.

Kevin Ripley was not a boy to be depressed for long. Already he had forgotten his unfortunate miss with the penalty kick (or, rather, he wouldn't allow himself to worry about it). He was thinking about how the team could be improved for the next match.

After pulling on his blue track-suit—like the others, he wouldn't change out of his football kit until he got home—he went over to Keith Nash

'I think you and I and Gary Ansell ought to have a meeting right away,' he said. 'We've got to sort things out for next week. I've got a few ideas. We can tell the rest of the team at the mid-week training session.'

'Okay,' Keith agreed. 'We'll make this an official selectors' meeting. There's something I want to say as well.'

Although Keith was the organizer and captain of Bank Vale United he didn't choose the team on his own. The previous season, their first in the Sunday Junior League, he had invited Kevin and Gary to join him as selectors. They were members of the original team and his closest friends. He had the final word, however, if Kevin and Gary disagreed about anything. That was his privilege as captain.

Keith made a point of thanking the rest of the team for turning out. He had a good word for all of them and didn't make any adverse criticisms of their play. He did add, though, that there would be a discussion of new tactics when they met for training on Tuesday evening.

When their team-mates had left the three

14

selectors strolled across the Common together. Kevin, who was in the middle, set the ball rolling.

'There've got to be some changes in this team, otherwise we'll never win anything. It was pitiful the way we threw the game away today.'

'We could have drawn it, you know,' Keith said mildly. Obviously he was referring to the missed penalty. But Kevin wasn't going to waste breath arguing about that.

'The defence isn't good enough,' he said bluntly.

'Who d'you mean?' Keith asked.

'Oh, those full-backs, Hallett and Parry. Simon Hallett couldn't tackle a good meal.'

'Well he hasn't got many teeth left since he fell off his bike,' Gary Ansell grinned. 'You can't blame him for that.'

'This is no time for joking, Gary,' Kevin said sternly. 'This is a serious business. Hallett's too soft—and Parry's got no positional sense. He just stands there, waiting for them to come to him instead of going after the man with the ball. That's no good. You've got to get stuck in at this game.'

'So what do you suggest?' Keith inquired.

'On Tuesday we shall have to give them a tough course in tackling—or a course in tough tackling, perhaps. I think we can sort that one out. Another thing: I think Harvey Slater has lost his confidence or something. Or maybe he's worried that he's not scoring as many goals as he did last season. When he gets in a good position he just belts the ball hard, hoping it'll go in, instead of picking his spot.

'I think Harvey should drop back into midfield. He can push out a good pass when he gives himself time and room.'

'Yes, I think that's a good idea,' Keith nodded. 'With his height Harvey could be a big help in defence, too. I was thinking of switching him before you mentioned it.'

'Well let's do it before it's too late,' Kevin went on. He doubted whether Keith had really been thinking about Harvey's position. But so long as Keith agreed with him that was all that mattered. 'I think we'll have to get rid of our inside-right, Andrew Cryer. He's useless. He's like his name— he makes you weep.'

'Who's making jokes now?' Gary put in.

Both Kevin and his captain ignored that remark.

'But we haven't got any spare players,' Keith pointed out. 'That's our real trouble: we've no reserves. And in a championship race a team is only as good as its reserves—that was what the manager of Albion was saying in the paper this week.'

'I know. I read it myself. But Albion can buy players when they need them. And that's what we've got to do, Keith.'

'Buy players!' Gary exploded. 'You must be nuts! There's no transfer system in the Sunday League. No team buys or sells players.'

'There's nothing in the rules to prevent it,' Kevin said calmly. 'I know, I've checked. If we have the money to buy a player and the team he plays for will sell him, well, that's okay. And if he's happy about it then he can start playing for us right away.'

Keith scratched his head through his close-cropped blond hair. 'But even if we wanted to buy a player we haven't got any money.'

'Oh, that can easily be arranged,' Kevin said confidently. 'There are always ways of raising money when you need to enter the transfer market.'

'Have you suddenly gone mad and been dreaming you're the manager of Arsenal or something?' Gary asked in mock-seriousness.

'I'm going to be a bank manager one day so I've taken the trouble to find out a few things about high finance,' Kevin told them. 'I believe in doing things properly.'

'Yes,' said Keith, who still seemed stunned by the idea of signing on a new player for a fee. 'But who do you think we should go for, Kevin? I mean, he's got to be terrific to cost real money.'

'I know the player we want. He plays inside-right for Ackton Wanderers. He's scored a hatful of goals for them this season. He's just what we need to give me some support up front.'

'A few moments ago you were saying our defence was bad,' Gary remarked. 'So what do you want to sign a forward for?'

'Because if we score more goals than our opponents we win the match. Attack is the best method of defence. And we haven't been scoring enough goals recently. You've not been hitting the net much yourself, Gary.'

'Well I haven't been getting much support

from my inside forwards, have I?' the right-winger grumbled.

'Exactly!' Kevin said triumphantly. 'Cryer's no good so we need to replace him. That's why I want to sign a good 'un like Nick Abel-Smith. You'll get some cracking passes from him. I know, I've seen him in action.'

'With a name like that he ought to be good. You sure you're not paying for his name?'

Kevin ignored that comment from Gary and turned to Keith. 'Well, what do you think, *captain*? Shall we sign him on? I tell you, he'll make a world of difference to United. With him we'd have the best forward line in the League.'

'How much will we have to pay for him?' Keith wanted to know. He was beginning to be impressed by the idea of entering the transfer market. United might get a lot of publicity out of such a move.

'Oh, I think we could get him for £1. And he'd be worth every penny of it.'

'A whole pound!' Gary exclaimed. 'We haven't got that sort of money. How are we going to get hold of all that?'

'It's not all that much, not when it's split up

among the members of the team,' Kevin said. 'It works out at only 10p each player. And 10p won't break anybody.'

'No it's less than 10p each because there are eleven of us,' Gary corrected him. 'So that's—'

'We can hardly ask Andy Cryer to contribute, can we?' Kevin said. 'It's not fair to ask him to help pay the transfer fee of the player who's going to replace him. So that's £1 between ten of us—10p each. If anybody needs a temporary loan I can arrange terms, you know.'

'I don't think that'll be necessary,' Keith said. 'I'm sure we can all find ways of getting hold of 10p. I'll put the idea up to the rest of the team on Tuesday night. I don't think anybody'll object if we three are in favour of the scheme.

'There's only one thing bothering me.'

'What's that?' Kevin asked, eager to help.

'Will Ackton Wanderers agree to sell—and will Abel-Smith want to play for us?'

'Oh, you don't have to worry about that,' Kevin assured him. 'I know how to fix things Nick will be scoring goals for us next Sunday.'

Two

Four members of the Bank Vale United team,
including Kevin Ripley, had no difficulty in paying their contributions to the transfer fee for Nick
Abel-Smith. They simply drew the money out of
their savings. In Kevin's case, however, he had to
ask his father to change a pound note.

Two other players asked their fathers for an
advance of their weekly pocket money. Both had
to argue a bit to convince the donors that the
matter was an urgent one but they got the money
in the end.

Johnny Butler had to earn his 10p the hard
way. Several times the milkman who called at his
house had asked Johnny if he'd like to earn some
spare cash. He wanted a boy to help him deliver
the milk bottles from house to house on his morning round. He was quite an old man and he said

that all this trailing up and down garden paths was wearing him out. Johnny wasn't keen on the idea because he hated getting out of bed early even at weekends.

Still, there seemed to be no other way of getting the money. So, much to the milkman's surprise, he agreed to help him out one morning. When he was told that it meant getting up at five o'clock he almost collapsed with shock. Johnny's mother didn't think there was any possibility of him waking on time. All the same, she agreed to lend him an alarm clock—and, to make sure he had the help of the loudest noise imaginable, she placed the clock inside an empty biscuit tin. 'The rattle that will make would awaken the dead,' she told him.

Johnny was dead to the world at five a.m. but the terrible clatter on his bedside table did the trick. He had to sit up to turn the thing off and save his eardrums from permanent damage.

After stumbling downstairs he made short work of the corned beef sandwiches his mother had left ready for him. He needed, she said, some solid food inside him if he was going out to work at that hour. He drank some milk and thought

about all the other bottles he was about to deliver.

Mr Hunt, the milkman, picked him up in his float a few minutes later and Johnny began the hardest work he'd ever known. At first he quite enjoyed the job. He tested his speed by running up the garden paths and sprinting back again to the gate. Mr Hunt said that if he carried on at that rate they'd be finished in no time. Johnny always responded to praise and he became quite skilled at setting down the full bottles and seizing the empties while still on the run.

Soon, however, his energy began to run out.

By six o'clock he was feeling quite exhausted. Often, too, he had trouble in opening garden gates. Some were fastened so securely he had to ask Mr Hunt to help by releasing the catches. Others seemed designed solely to trap his fingers. Johnny collected several bruises.

It was after Johnny had dropped a couple of bottles—unluckily, they were both full ones—that Mr Hunt decided that his young helper had done enough.

'Oh no, I can carry on a bit longer,' Johnny said bravely, although he doubted whether he could walk another yard. Mr Hunt, however, delivered the boy to his own gate and gave him 50p—twice the amount Johnny had been promised.

So, feeling richer than he'd ever been in his life, Johnny pocketed the cash and carried three bottles of milk to his own front door, his final delivery of the day. His mother's first remark was: 'You look as though you ought to drink one of those bottles right away.'

'No thanks, I'd rather have coffee,' said Johnny, who ate a huge breakfast while working out how he was going to spend the 40p that would be left over when he'd paid his share of the transfer fee.

Harvey Slater spent part of the same morning trying to decide which football programmes in his collection he should sell. He had been a Leeds United fan for more than two seasons and the Leeds programmes were the pride of his collection. Although he had been to Elland Road, Leeds, only twice he obtained their programmes by exchanges with other collectors. Harvey had several pen friends in various parts of the country to whom he sent programmes of his local First Division team, Albion. In return he received programmes of matches played by Leeds, Manchester United and Norwich City.

Sometimes he bought programmes of international and other important matches and the centrepiece of his collection was the programme for the World Cup Final between England and West Germany at Wembley in 1966. Harvey would rather sell his life than sell that souvenir.

Still, he needed to get hold of 10p quickly, so he had to sell something. He thought about it for a very long time. At last, he made up his mind. He would sell some of the Manchester United programmes. There was always a good market for them among his pals at school. He thought he wouldn't miss too badly some of the programmes of the Reds' less important matches.

Harvey was sorry to let them go but he realized that the other United—Bank Vale—came first. His own team needed his 10p contribution to the purchase of Nick Abel-Smith. Harvey only hoped their new player would be worth his great sacrifice.

Gary Ansell had to wait until his father came home that evening before he could start to earn the 10p he needed. Although Mr Ansell was quite a keen motorist he didn't bother to keep his car very clean; at least, he never cleaned it himself. Now and again he took it to a car-wash but he didn't have it polished.

Once Gary had mentioned to his father that the car looked filthy. 'Oh, that doesn't matter,' Godfrey Ansell replied. 'If you watch a rugby match you'll see that the best players always look as if they've just had a mud-bath. It's what's under the bonnet that counts. Anyway, I drive so many miles in all weathers that to keep my chariot clean I'd have to wash it every day. Waste of money, that.'

In spite of that point of view, Gary hoped to persuade his father to allow him to clean the car that evening. For a modest payment, of course. Only 10p. He had worked out a clever plan of persuasion.

'I say, Dad,' he began when his father arrived home. 'Did you know that cars which are all smart and shiny show up better at night and don't get involved in as many accidents as dirty-looking cars? I was reading about it in a paper. A clean car is a safe car—that's what somebody called a spokesman said.'

'Oh, yes,' Mr Ansell answered, showing some interest. He was quite keen on road safety. 'What paper was that in? I didn't see it.'

'I don't remember which paper it was,' Gary replied with absolute truth since he had invented the story. 'But it seems sensible. So can I clean your car tonight for you? I don't want you to be killed in a road accident because another motorist didn't see your car coming.'

'Certainly, certainly,' Mr Ansell agreed with enthusiasm. 'I'm glad to know you're thinking of your old Dad's welfare, Gary. You deserve a reward for good thinking. What would you like?'

28

'Oh. . . .' Gary hesitated. 'Well, how about some money? Twenty pence would be very nice. I mean, that's what it would cost you at the car-wash, isn't it?'

Gary was thinking he might as well make a profit if he had the chance. Then he noticed a look of suspicion on his father's face. He began to wonder whether he'd been too clever.

'Tell me, Gary, what exactly do you want the money for?' Godfrey Ansell demanded. 'I know your cunning ways. Come on, out with it. This safety business is all an angle to get something, isn't it?'

'Oh no, Dad, not really. It's all true. But, well, yes I do need some money. It's something to do with United—it's secret actually. But, honestly, we do need some money—and I wanted to earn it.'

'I see. But, you know Gary, if you want money for new kit or anything like that I'd gladly have given it to you without all this rigmarole about cleaning cars. After all, I'm one of United's sup-porters.'

That was quite true. Although he was an ex-rugby player Godfrey Ansell had become a keen soccer fan during United's first season in the Sunday League. He went to watch their matches when he had the time and he gave Gary a lot of encouragement.

'So if it's money for United,' he went on, 'you're welcome to it.'

'Oh, *thanks*, Dad, thanks a lot....'

'But,' Mr Ansell went on with a grin on his face, 'as you've also offered to clean my car to save my life I don't want to stop your good deed. So get on with it—and when you've finished you can have your money.'

With a sigh, Gary departed to fetch a bucket of warm water. He decided that sometimes it was best just to say what you wanted and not try to be too clever.

Keith Nash shared that point of view. The easiest way of getting the money he needed was to ask his mother for it and tell her exactly why he wanted it. That approach had usually worked in the past.

So he told her that he needed 10p 'to help United out of a jam. All the lads,' he explained, 'are putting 10p each into the kitty. So I've got to do the same.'

'Well, I'll think about it,' Mrs Nash replied in a rather unconcerned way. She seemed about to change the subject.

'Oh, but Mum, it's an emergency. Very urgent,' Keith persisted. 'I mean, I've got to put my share into the kitty tomorrow.'

Mrs Nash sighed. 'Money doesn't just grow on trees, you know, Keith. I give you what we can afford each week. I know it's not much but, well, your Dad and I have a lot of expenses. And then it's my turn for the flowers at chapel this week.'

It annoyed Keith that his mother was so keen on the chapel. He had to go with her each Sunday morning and he thought that was a waste of valuable training time. On the other hand, she didn't object to his playing football in the afternoon; in fact, she showed a lot of interest in United.

'Anyway, what are you all going to do with this money if you get it?' she wanted to know. 'Buy a new ball or something?'

'Not really. Actually, we're going to buy a player, so we need the money for his transfer fee.'

Mrs Nash looked as amazed as she sounded. '*Buy* a player! But you're all amateurs. Only professional teams *buy* players. Keith, this doesn't sound a very healthy attitude to me. You sound as if United are in a commercial business. I can't approve of that.'

'Oh, it's not as bad as it sounds, Mum,' her son pointed out desperately. 'It's only that we need a new player rather badly and the only way to get a good one is to pay a transfer fee.

'I mean,' he added shrewdly, 'we've got to compensate the team that's losing him. That's only fair, isn't it?'

'I suppose so,' Mrs Nash agreed, without sounding as if she meant it. 'Who is this boy, anyway? The new player you want, I mean?'

'His name is Nick Abel-Smith. I've never seen him but Kevin Ripley reckons he's a great player.'

'Oh, then I think he must be Shirley Abel-Smith's boy. It's not a common name. She's a very nice person, I like her enormously. She's a big church worker. Oh, well that's different. Her son should be an asset to your team.'

She took her purse out of her handbag and searched for a 10p-piece. Mentally Keith offered up a prayer of thanks. He thought it was fully justified on this occasion.

'Here you are,' his mother said. 'But don't ask for anything like this again. It mustn't become a habit. One new player is enough for any team— especially if he's as good as Kevin says he is.'

'Thanks, Mum, you're a pal,' Keith said, pocketing the coin with relief. It would have been awful if United's captain had been the only player who didn't contribute to the transfer fee.

Kevin had the whole pound in his pocket the following morning when he arrived at a school playing field on the other side of the town. He had arranged to see John Storton, the captain of Ackton Wanderers, and Nick Abel-Smith to complete the details of the transfer.

'Have you got the money?' was the first question John Storton asked as Kevin strolled up. Kevin nodded and handed over a 50p-piece.

'Hey, that's only half what you promised,' John protested. 'Where's the rest? Come on, hand it over.'

'Not yet,' Kevin replied calmly. 'You'll get the other 50p when Nick's scored ten goals for us. That's how all the best transfers are arranged. Payment by results, you know.'

John seemed to be on the point of exploding but Nick, who hadn't said a word so far, reached out to shake Kevin's hand.

'The deal's okay by me,' he said. 'Don't worry, John, you'll get your money in a couple of weeks. I expect I'll get a hat-trick each week. The opposition won't know what's hit them.'

There was no smile on Nick's thin face, and certainly none in his dark eyes, as he said that.

Obviously he meant every word. Kevin wasn't going to dispute it. The last thing he wanted to do was ruin a new team-mate's confidence. In any case, he'd seen Nick in action for his school team and he knew that this boy was a natural goal-grabber.

'I suppose you haven't managed to collect the other 50p,' John muttered.

'Oh yes I have,' Kevin replied, displaying the coin. 'And I'm going to put it to work before I have to pay it over to you. I'm going to lend it out at interest to earn a few pence. That's the way to earn more money.'

'The way you're going on you'll finish up as manager of Manchester United or running the Bank of England,' John said with a sneer.

'Both, I expect,' Kevin answered quietly. 'I shan't stop making money just because I've become a millionaire.

'Anyway,' he went on, 'we must be off. Nick and I have a lot of thinking to do. We've got to work out our tactics for tomorrow's match against Rosehill Athletic. So come on, Nick, let's go and do some planning at my place.'

Three

When Kevin Ripley introduced Nick Abel-Smith to his new team-mates just before the start of Sunday's game he also announced that he himself was going to be United's new centre-forward. That was not something he had discussed with either Gary Ansell or Keith Nash. It was a decision he had taken entirely on his own.

As captain, Keith felt he ought to have been consulted. However, he decided not to say anything. He didn't want there to be any arguments within the team before or during a match United just had to win. All the same, he had the feeling that he was being pushed into the background and that Kevin was trying to take over the running of the team. He would have a word with him about that when the game finished.

Gary, on the other hand, believed in saying immediately what he thought.

36

'Hey, who's idea is that?' he asked Kevin. 'You're not tall enough to be a centre-forward —even Nick's taller than you.'

'Only by half an inch,' Kevin replied, as precise as always when he was quoting facts. 'And, anyway, that doesn't matter. I can jump higher than he can. If you send over some good centres from the right wing I'll be there to nod 'em in, young Gary.'

Gary, who didn't like to be reminded that he was a year younger than Kevin, still wasn't satisfied.

'But what about Harvey Slater? Where's he going to play?' he demanded. 'You can't start switching the team around like this without letting everybody know.'

Although Harvey was present he didn't say a word. He never had much to say for himself at any time—unlike Kevin who seldom stopped talking.

'I've had a word with Harvey,' Kevin explained as if Harvey were nowhere to be seen. 'He's quite happy to play at inside-left in a midfield role. He'll be pushing the ball through for Nick and me. I reckon Harvey and Keith'll give us a good service, won't you, lads?'

Keith was so surprised to be treated just like any other member of the team by Kevin that he merely nodded.

'Good,' Kevin said. 'That's settled then. All we've got to do now is pulverize Rosehill Athletic. Nick's seen 'em play before and he says they're a pushover. Right, Nick?'

'No trouble,' Nick agreed. 'No trouble at all. Just keep bashing the ball upfield and Kevin and I'll do the rest.'

'Oh, thanks very much. Thanks *very much*,' Gary said in his very best sarcastic manner. 'It's good of you to let us all take part in the same game.'

'Okay, lads,' Keith said to cool things down and show that he was still the captain of Bank Vale United. 'Let's get out there and start winning again. This is the most important match of the season as far as we're concerned. We *must* win it.'

Rosehill Athletic didn't start the match like a team who were going to be a pushover for the opposition. From the kick-off Langton, their burly centre-forward, exchanged passes with his inside-left and then stormed into the heart of the United defence. Harvey Slater, who'd already dropped back, was the first player he thrust aside and when Keith tried to tackle him Langton's weight was too much for the United captain. Langton strode on with plenty of team-mates up in support.

Simon Hallett, who had been practising his tackling techniques all week, wasn't going to allow the size of Athletic's centre-forward to put him off. He rushed in furiously to block Langton's path to goal. Langton side-stepped him like a man avoiding a banana skin on a pavement.

Alex Hornsey was showing signs of desperate anxiety on his goal-line. The sight of Langton bearing down on the goal-mouth was a pretty terrifying one. Alex thought he ought to come out, although he was sure he'd be safer where he was.

By now Keith Nash had recovered his balance and was giving chase as hard as he could. He had just caught up with the opposing centre-forward when Langton, quite delicately, turned the ball sideways to Minter, his inside-left. Minter now had a clear sight of goal and, choosing his spot well, he cracked the ball into the net just inside the near post. Hornsey still hadn't moved.

The unselfish Langton shook Minter's hand and turned to trot back to the centre-circle. United were a goal down before even one of their players had touched the ball.

'Well, if this lot are a pushover all I can say is I'm glad we're not playing a good side,' Gary muttered to Keith Nash.

'Don't say anything like that to Kevin,' the skipper warned him. 'I don't want any trouble in the team. So come on, let's get down to it. We're not beaten yet.'

It appeared that Kevin and Nick had said a word to each other. They stood side by side, waiting for the signal to start the game again. Kevin was gritting his teeth. He was thinking of all the horrible things he'd like to do to certain United defenders. Nick, on the other hand, looked quite relaxed. He wasn't bothered by weaknesses in his team's defence. He was perfectly confident he would score the necessary goals to put his side in front.

When the ball came to him he jinked to one side to avoid a tackle by the enthusiastic Langton.

Then, keeping the ball at his feet, he slipped away towards the right wing. Gary was already on the move. Anticipating a pass he accelerated along the flank.

Nick, however, cut the ball back inside to Kevin who screened it well as a Rosehill defender tried to bundle it away from him. Kevin was usually at his best when someone was trying to take the ball off him. This time he turned a complete circle before moving away with the ball. To Keith's surprise, Kevin didn't try to keep possession the next time he was challenged. Choosing his moment well, he flicked the ball back to Nick, who was no longer being shadowed.

This time Gary was certain he was going to get a pass. He was wrong. Once again, the ball went back to Kevin, now on the edge of the penalty area.

That was really what the Rosehill defence had expected. Two players moved in on Kevin at the same moment and between them they forced the ball from him. They hadn't time to clear it before Kevin fell dramatically to the ground. He began to writhe in agony as he clutched his left knee.

The referee stopped the game and, looking

quite alarmed, went over to examine Kevin's injury. There was no blood in evidence but Kevin protested furiously about the 'rotten kick on the knee' he'd received from one of the Athletic players. He pointed out the culprit to the referee, who stalked off to caution the offender.

'I didn't do nothing!' the boy insisted. He presented a wonderful picture of innocence. It wasn't an act because he really hadn't done anything wrong. 'Ripley just fell over me.'

Unfortunately for him, the referee didn't believe him. Kevin had been so convincing.

Instead, he awarded United a free kick.

Kevin made a remarkably quick recovery. Without so much as a limp in his stride, he placed the ball and then sidefooted it to Nick. United's inside-right hit the ball first time. Rosehill's defence had not lined up properly and there was a gap wide enough for Nick to shoot through.

The ball was only inches wide of the target. It thudded against the near upright. The goalkeeper could only look on in amazement at the speed of the shot. From the ricochet the ball was scrambled away but already Kevin's new signing had impressed his team-mates.

From that moment both teams began to produce some very lively football. The handful of supporters who had come to watch had plenty to cheer about and the noise they made encouraged the players greatly.

During Rosehill's attacks it was Edward Lancaster, United's young left-half, who was doing most to keep them at bay. A well-built boy for his age with freckles and a mop of sandy-coloured hair that was beyond his control, he was tackling like a tiger. In practice sessions he had been paying close attention to Kevin's advice. He admired

44

Kevin's play and was determined to be as good on the ball as United's new centre-forward. While Hallett and Parry had only been half-hearted about trying to improve their defensive play Edward Lancaster forgot nothing he learned. Like Keith and Gary he practised on his own with a ball on the Common in his spare time. His skills were developing week by week.

Just before half-time it was Edward who set up the chance for United to grab the equalizer. Intercepting a pass intended for Langton he set off up the field at tremendous speed. Harvey Slater signalled for the ball and Edward banged it across to him—but didn't stop running. Harvey, who had a keen eye for an opening, saw what was happening. He let a defender approach him and then booted the ball over the boy's head for Edward to chase.

That was just what Edward wanted. Still moving at top speed he reached the ball before anyone else. Although Kevin was calling for the ball, as usual, he was well marked. So Edward ignored him and hammered a pass towards Nick Abel-Smith.

Nick moved to take it on his instep. For once

he had plenty of space to move in and he made the most of it. He reached the edge of the penalty area without meeting any interference. By now Kevin was also running hard. Nick flicked the ball to him as a defender closed in—and then stepped past the boy in anticipation of getting a return pass.

Once Kevin had any chance at all of scoring a goal he wasn't willing to pass that chance to anyone else. He lashed his shot towards the net and it would undoubtedly have gone in—if the goalkeeper hadn't been in the way. The goalie fumbled the ball and allowed it to bounce out of his arms. Kevin was following up for just that sort of situation. Nick, however, was there first. With one simple push from the side of his foot he turned the ball into the net. Kevin would have tried to break the net from that position.

Nick accepted Kevin's congratulations very calmly. When Kevin pointed out that he himself deserved the goal Nick didn't say anything. He might, though, have pointed out that Kevin ought to show a little more accuracy in his shooting.

Instead, he trotted over to Edward Lancaster. 'That was very smart work on your part,

Edward,' he said. 'Keep it up, lad.'

Edward's face lit up with pleasure. Up to that moment, none of his team-mates had given him any praise. Now he was determined to do even better if possible. He was very glad to think he was going to get on well with Kevin's new friend.

At half-time Keith delivered one of his usual pep talks and urged his co-defenders to keep Langton and Minter under control. He had already saluted Nick's goal and now he suggested that the forwards would do even better if they gave the wingers a bit more of the ball. 'Gary Ansell didn't get a sniff of it in the first half,' he pointed out.

Gary, who was feeling very neglected indeed, agreed with that. 'Yeah, push it about a bit, will you, Nick? I mean, I am playing in this game, you know.'

'Athletic are stronger on your wing,' Nick answered quietly. 'We've got to attack down the left. That's where we can rip 'em open. If Edward comes up more in support we'll carve 'em up.'

'That's just what I think,' Kevin nodded. 'Let's concentrate on the left. Johnny's got the speed to get round the back.'

Gary felt insulted. He knew he was at least as fast as Johnny Butler. After all, he held the record for the 100 yards at his school, Scale Hill Comprehensive. If they'd only give him the ball he reckoned he could do just as much damage down his wing. But before he could say so the referee was ready to start the second half.

Fired with enthusiasm, Edward rushed up to join in United's first attack and contributed a good pass to Johnny Butler. The little winger sped away down the touchline until a well-timed sliding tackle robbed him of the ball. By the time Johnny had got to his feet the ball was in play again.

Edward had sprinted for the ball and taken a very quick throw-in. Rosehill were caught unawares by the speed of his reaction. For once they hadn't a man covering Kevin Ripley. It was Kevin who received the ball from Edward's throw and he darted away with it at his toes. He spotted that Nick was racing into the middle of the penalty box.

Kevin hit the ball hard in the direction of his friend. It bounced only once and as it rose again

48

Nick swung his left foot and rocketed the ball into the top of the net.

By any reckoning, it was a marvellous goal. Nick possessed the confidence in himself and the positioning sense to be in the right place at the right time and to shoot on sight.

Once again, he shrugged off the congratulations of his colleagues. It was his job to score goals and he expected to score them. He didn't think he'd done anything particularly brilliant.

All the same, his team-mates were thrilled. Athletic had been giving them such a hard time that few thought they had a chance of winning the match. Now United were in front—and they were determined to stay there.

Nick made a point of having another word with Edward Lancaster. 'That was quick thinking on your part, Edward,' he said. 'Most players are very sloppy about taking a throw-in. They waste time. You gave us just the opening we needed by taking a quick throw.'

With that second helping of praise Nick Abel-Smith had made a friend for life in Edward Lancaster. The carrot-haired half-back was overjoyed.

Athletic were by no means finished because they were a goal down. They stormed back into the attack like a wind that had been gathering its forces just over the horizon. They were determined to sweep everything and everyone out of their way on the road to goal.

Harvey Slater dropped back to help United's hard-pressed defence. His height was useful for Rosehill tried to pump the ball into the air towards Langton. By now rain was falling heavily and players on both sides were feeling the effects of what had been a tough struggle for supremacy.

Both Keith Nash, one of the fittest boys on the field, and Simon Hallett felt they were being rushed off their feet. Their boots seemed to be filled with lead weights. Once Keith was so slow to make a tackle that Minter had all the time he needed to look round for support. That almost led to an equalizing goal as Langton came up to hit a fierce drive that Alex Hornsey just managed to clutch at the second attempt. Then, after kicking the ball to safety during another attack, Harvey Slater had to stop to get his breath back.

Nick Abel-Smith made no effort to assist his

defence. His job was to stay up-field—and he stayed there. He didn't receive another pass before the match ended but that didn't bother him. All that mattered to him was that United should win. To Nick the margin of victory was unimportant: in his eyes a 2-1 victory was just as good as a 6-0 thrashing. That was one thing on which he and Kevin disagreed. Kevin wanted to pulverize every team they met.

When the final whistle blew most of the United players had just enough breath left to whoop with delight. After so little success recently it was good to be on the winning side again. Keith congratulated each of them on his performance. He didn't believe in being too tough with his players however badly things might be going; but he always gave praise and encouragement where he could.

Nick, however, was one member of the team who wasn't satisfied with the way the match had gone. He said that United should have created chances to score more goals during the last quarter-of-an-hour. Rosehill, he went on, had pushed so many men up into attack that there'd been great gaps in their defence.

'But,' he added severely, 'none of our defenders had enough energy left to give us forwards the ball. That's because most of you aren't fit. You haven't trained properly so you can't last out a game. If the rain had come earlier to make conditions on the pitch worse, well, you'd all have been half-dead ... washed-up ... finished. Then Rosehill would have won easily. Now they are fit, very fit. I reckon we were lucky to beat 'em today.'

Keith looked stunned. Nobody had ever accused him before of not being fit. He prided himself on all the training he did. It was true that at the moment he did feel pretty tired. But he wasn't going to admit that to Nick.

Gary was furious. He wasn't going to let Nick get away with insulting him a second time.

'I'm fitter than I've ever been in my life,' he declared. 'It'd be funny if I wasn't. I haven't had any exercise today. Nobody gave me a proper pass at any time during the game. So I could run ten miles this minute and not feel a thing.'

The sarcasm had no effect on Nick. 'You were our secret weapon,' he said, and his face was perfectly straight. 'We were keeping your speed

in reserve until we needed it. But we didn't need
it so that's okay.'

He turned slightly to face the other boys.
'Anyway, let's forget Gary's moaning. All I'm
interested in at the moment is fitness—the fitness
of our team. If we aren't fit we're going to get
beaten—often.'

'What do you suggest we do, then?' Keith
asked. 'Run a mile up the road and back again?
Or stand on our heads for half-an-hour? Or—'

'Not quite,' Nick replied, cutting him off. 'But
I think we should do what the professional footballers do—run up and down the terraces to
strengthen leg muscles and build up stamina.
That's what we lack: stamina.'

'Oh, yes,' Gary said with mock-cheerfulness.
'And where do we do this running up and down
terraces—at Albion's ground?'

'Of course,' Nick answered.

That was not at all what Gary had expected.
He'd thought his joke would be treated as a joke.
But Nick seemed quite serious about it.

'But how are we going to do that?' Gary was
forced to ask.

'We break in one night, that's how. It's quite

easy. I've done it hundreds of times.'

'Honest?' Keith was impressed. The idea appealed to him but he wasn't entirely sure that Nick wasn't making it up.

'Oh, yes. I go over the wall at the same place every time. Nobody's ever spotted me. They only expect people to try and get into the ground on match days, not at night during the middle of the week.'

'But how will we see what we're doing when we do get in?' Edward wanted to know. 'I mean, won't it be dark?'

'Not if we pick a moonlit night,' Nick replied. 'There's a full moon next Thursday. I know, I've looked it up. I'd've been going on my own, anyway. Now that I've seen that you lot need to get fit I think we all ought to go.'

Keith didn't need to suggest that they voted on the matter. He could tell that most of his team-mates were already looking forward to the adventure.

Four

One by one the members of Bank Vale United
assembled in the shadow of a huge, empty ware-
house on Causley Street. They had been told by
Nick to meet at seven o'clock but most of them
were there several minutes earlier. All were
wearing track-suits and plimsolls. Some had
abandoned their homework halfway through,
others hadn't even started theirs. Some were
nervous, a few were eager to try anything once
and only Simon Hallett was scared of what might
happen if they were caught. His father was a
policeman and so he knew all about the penalties
of breaking the law.

Nick was in charge because only he knew how
they were going to get into the ground. It was
Keith, however, who issued the orders about not
talking loudly and doing what they were told

once they were over the wall. He was the captain of the team and he wanted Nick and Kevin to remember that. He wasn't going to allow them to think that he could be ordered about at any time.

On a signal from Nick they sneaked across the street and raced for the shelter of the high wall behind the main terrace. Crouched low and in single file they made their way to the big car park at the far end of the street. The moon was hidden by a bank of cloud and it was very dark indeed. But, as Nick had pointed out, that was all in their favour. He forecast that there would soon be a clear sky. He seemed to know quite a lot about weather conditions.

The car park was not as empty as they'd expected it to be. Several cars, including some big lorries, had been left there. One car at least was occupied. They spotted the flare of a match as someone lit a cigarette.

'Do you think that's the police, watching out for us?' Johnny Butler whispered to Nick.

'Not a chance,' Nick replied confidently. 'It's just some bloke and his girl friend. This is a favourite spot for courting couples.'

Like most members of the team, Johnny instantly accepted anything he was told by Nick. Their star forward always seemed to know what he was talking about.

Simon, of course, was alert for any signs of police activity. He was concentrating so hard on trying to spot policemen that he almost fell over a couple of bricks someone had forgotten to pick up. In the stillness of the gloomy car park that made quite a lot of noise. The United team froze to the spot. Most of them were really frightened now.

'You careless idiot!' Nick hissed at Simon who was shivering with fear. 'Watch what you're doing. We don't want to be stopped before we even get into the ground.'

'Sorry, Nick,' mumbled Simon. 'But it's so dark.'

'Get some glasses then—or shove off home.'

There was nothing Simon would have liked better than to return home but he didn't want to be the only member of the team who missed an important training session. If he chickened-out now he'd certainly be dropped for the next match.

So the unhappy Simon crept along on tip-toe behind the other boys. They stopped only when they reached the far end of the car park. They were still behind the main terrace. Next to the last pair of turnstile entrances was a big notice board. The display poster on the board announced details of Albion's next home match against Derby County the following Saturday.

'This is it,' Nick murmured. 'Now just watch me. It's easy if you do what I do. Johnny, you'd better come next because you're the smallest. Harvey can give you a hand up. Okay?'

He didn't wait for any answer. Grasping one of the metal pegs that supported the wooden board he hauled himself on to the lower ledge.

The pegs had not been driven very deeply into the brickwork of the wall and several stuck out a couple of inches or so. Using the pegs as footrests Nick was able to scale the wall quite easily. Once he'd reached the top of the board he had a ledge wide enough to stand on. From that point he could pull himself on to the top of the wall. Luckily, there was no broken glass there to keep out intruders.

Nick waited until Johnny Butler was within reach. He leaned down to give him a helping hand. Then Nick scrambled along the wall until

he was above one of the turnstile entrances. He was able to descend by using the wooden framework of the doorway and a couple of bricks that protruded from the wall.

Keith, as the captain, was the last to make the ascent. Simon Hallett was just ahead of him and Keith wanted to make sure that his team-mate didn't make any mistakes. In fact, Simon showed a lot of agility and went over the top with ease. 'Good for him,' Keith thought.

'Hey, that was great!' Edward Lancaster said with enthusiasm as he turned to look at the route he'd just taken. 'Maybe we ought to come in this way again when we come to see Albion.'

'Not a chance,' Nick replied, quashing that idea very swiftly. 'On match days there are millions of cops everywhere. And, anyway, the grown-ups wouldn't let you. If they're paying their entrance money they want you to do the same.'

'I want to go to the gents,' Simon announced. 'Yeah, so do I,' Alex Hornsey said. Together they hurried away to the urinal beside the turnstile entrance.

'That's what happens when you get scared,' Nick grinned as he watched them disappear.

'Couple of softies, those two.'

He led the way up the steps to the top of the banking on which the terraces were built. When they reached the summit they could look down over the stairways and crush barriers to the playing area. At that moment the moon emerged from behind a cloud bank and softly lit up the pitch. Although part of it was in the shadow cast by the roof of the main stand they could make out both sets of goal posts and the white markings.

Each United player gazed with a sense of wonder at one of the most famous football grounds in Britain. Each had watched Albion play there many times but never before had they seen it under such conditions: empty and yet alive with shadows, silent and yet full of mysterious drama.

The imagination of each of them was stirred. They were playing for Albion in a sixth-round F.A. Cup-tie against Manchester United. Wembley was only another 90 minutes' away. The ground was packed, the gates were closed. One minute to the final whistle, the score still 0-0. The ball comes over into the United penalty area

—and each of them banged it into the net for the winning goal.

'Right,' said Nick crisply, returning to reality. 'Let's get cracking. We can't stay here all night.'

He sorted the players out into two groups with himself in charge of one and Keith the other. They made their way to the foot of the terrace and there the groups split up. One player from each section was going to compete against his opposite number. Together they would race up the stairway to a given point, turn, and then dash back down again. They would run it like a relay race so that as soon as one boy returned his team-mate would set off.

'Put all you've got into this—and no slacking,' Nick said. 'It's hard work but it's good for you. Right—GO!'

Gary Ansell and Harvey Slater were the first pair. Although Harvey was the taller and stronger they were well matched. Gary was fast and nippy; Harvey's long stride was not an advantage in climbing steps at speed.

At the point where they turned—marked by a crush barrier that almost jutted out into the stair-way—it was neck-and-neck. As they came rushing down side by side their team-mates wanted to yell their encouragement. But Nick had insisted there should be no noise at any time once they were inside the ground.

Gary's greater speed down the last few steps gave his team a narrow lead. Alex Hornsey bounded away ahead of Edward Lancaster. As it turned out, neither team was able to keep in front for long; they were well matched. Because there were eleven players one had to stand down for the first race and Nick said that as he was the fittest he didn't need to take part. That comment had drawn a sharp look from Keith but he hadn't objected.

The final pair were Keith and Johnny Butler. Keith really could move when he wanted to and he streaked away. It was important to him to show Nick how fit he was. At the turn he was several steps ahead and he kept his lead until the end.

'Well done, lads,' Nick said. 'But I can see from the way you're all panting like mad that you needed some stiff training. We'll have five minutes' rest and then see if my team can win the second race. As you were the last runner,

Johnny, you can sit this one out. I'll go first against Harvey.'

Nick again gave the signal to start and before the word was out of his mouth he was leaping up the first step. Harvey was slowly away because he wasn't ready. United's new goal-scoring star obviously possessed good acceleration. One reason for his success in turning half chances into goals was that he could move so quickly into the penalty box. Keith guessed that Nick wouldn't be so fast over a longer distance. And he was right.

Although he wasn't by any means the fastest runner in Keith's team Harvey had practically caught up with Nick when their leg of the race was over. Nick, however, didn't let that worry him. He was still breathing quite evenly and showing no signs of his exertions. He hoped somebody would point out how fit he was. Kevin obliged.

'Great stuff, Nick. You look fit enough to do that again without getting out of breath.'

Nick just nodded—and turned his attention to the next pair of runners. Gary was running for his team against Simon Hallett. Keith had changed the order of his side because he wanted to keep his fastest runners for the finish. In this second race the rule about silence had been forgotten. Both teams had started to cheer on their own runners.

'Come on, Simon!' Edward Lancaster was yelling. 'Don't take a rest halfway! Keep running.'

Simon didn't like to be accused of not trying his hardest. He knew he wasn't particularly good at anything but at least he always made an effort. Already Gary was several steps ahead of him. For the first time a gap had opened up between the two teams. Simon didn't want his side to lose. So he would have to try to go faster.

Desperately, he tried to increase his speed. But rhythm is essential when running up or down steps. Simon lost his rhythm—and then missed his footing. He over-balanced completely, fell forward and then began to roll down the steps at a quite frightening speed. He was going so fast he almost caught up with Gary Ansell.

Simon had started to yell quite frantically at the start of his fall. But the bumping he received on each step knocked the breath out of him. It was Keith who halted Simon's disastrous progress. He rushed forward to stop him rolling any further. With Gary's assistance he hauled the battered full-back to his feet.

He seemed quite dazed, perhaps even surprised to find that he was still alive. Then he began to cry, very noisily. Keith had noticed the blood on Simon's right-knee and he dragged a hanky from his pocket. As he bent to dab the blood away Simon noticed what was happening.

'Oh, oh, OH!' he wailed. 'I've bust my knee. It's broken, I know it's broken.'

'Don't be daft,' Nick said sharply. 'If you'd broken it you wouldn't be able to stand on it. Just a graze—that's all. Stick that hanky round it, Keith. It'll stop the bleeding.'

'Leave it alone,' Simon roared. 'I'll have to go to hospital. I might have got poison in the wound. It's probably infected.'

That remark stopped Keith from taking any further action. Medical terms always impressed him. He'd had several illnesses himself. Unlike Simon, however, he'd never been in hospital. Perhaps Simon really knew what he was talking about.

66

'Sounds like you've got trouble,' someone said, breaking the silence. 'Maybe I can help.'

It was an adult's voice and the United players swung round to see who had spoken. Looking up at them from the running track round the pitch was a tall, young man: a man most of them recognized immediately.

'It's Dave Archer!' Gary Ansell gasped. Dave Archer, Albion's brilliant winger with the goal-scoring touch, was his hero. Neither the gloom nor the fact that Dave was dressed in ordinary clothes raised any doubts in his mind. It was instant identification.

'Oh, hello, Dave,' Nick said casually. 'Glad to see you.'

'I heard all this noise from the other side of the park so I came over to see what was going on,' Dave said. 'What's happened?'

'Young Hallett here fell down the steps and knocked his knee,' Nick explained. 'He's been making a lot of fuss but it's nothing really. Just a scratch and a drop of blood.'

'It could be dangerous if its infected,' Simon protested. 'You shouldn't take risks with an injury.'

'Quite right,' Dave agreed, much to everyone's surprise. 'You ought to have it looked at right away. You're in luck because Ricky Bartlett, our trainer, is in the treatment room right now. I've just been seeing him about a pulled muscle I got in our last match. So he can have a look at you, son. Come on over to the offices. You other lads give him a hand.'

Keith and Gary and Alex Hornsey leapt to obey. Simon had never received such attention from his pals in his life. With his arms round their shoulders he allowed them to half-carry, half-pull him across the famous playing pitch. For a moment he forgot his injury and imagined he was an Albion player being chaired off the field in triumph.

In awe the United players trooped down the tunnel and into the corridor beneath the main grandstand. Dave Archer led the way to a gleaming-white treatment room equipped with what looked like an operating table and rows and rows of silver instruments.

Ricky Bartlett was a grey-haired man with a kind face and after a few words from Dave he asked Simon to lie on the table so that he could attend to him. There wasn't a murmur from Simon as Mr Bartlett cleaned away the blood and dust from the wound, applied some ointment and then a bandage. Wide-eyed, Simon was looking round the treatment room and thinking that it was even better than the hospitals he'd attended. Best of all, he was being treated by the man who looked after the Albion players.

Meanwhile, Dave was chatting to the other United players. Nick was the one who answered most of his questions. Both Gary and Keith were envious of the familiar way Nick talked to their hero. He kept calling him 'Dave' and they wished they dare do the same; but somehow it didn't seem right when they were actually with him. So they addressed him as 'Mr Archer'.

Nick was perfectly truthful about how they had got into the ground—and the method they'd used seemed to amuse Dave Archer. He didn't tell them off for breaking in—and breaking the law. He said he admired their enthusiasm and he hoped their extra training would help them to win more often. He asked a lot of questions about United and again it was Nick who did most of the talking. Keith felt it might sound big-headed if he pointed out that he, not Nick, was the captain.

Gary desperately wanted to say something to his hero. But suddenly he found he had nothing to say. All the questions he'd thought of in his room at night when he'd imagined just such a meeting as this had gone. He'd dried up completely. Of course, what he really wanted was to have Dave Archer talk to *him*. But although Dave glanced at the other boys from time to time he seemed to be talking directly to Nick.

With a helping hand from Mr Bartlett Simon climbed off the treatment table and tested his injured leg. 'I haven't put the bandage on tightly,' the trainer told him. 'You must give your knee a bit of exercise because we don't want it to stiffen up. You should be fine in a couple of days. Lads of your age soon recover from a knock.'

'Will I be able to play on Sunday, sir?' Simon inquired.

'Oh, I should think so. But that will depend on how the knee feels to you. Only you can tell how fit you feel.'

Gary seized his chance. 'Will you be fit to play for Albion on Saturday, Mr Archer?'

'I expect so, son. There's nothing much wrong

with me, is there, Ricky?' He grinned at Mr Bartlett and got an answering thumbs-up from the trainer. 'Anyway, I must be off now—and I think you lads should be on your way home as well. You don't want to overdo this training business, you know. An hour at a time's enough, I reckon. Regular training is the secret—a bit every day instead of all at one go.

'Well, you didn't come in through the players' entrance but I think that's the way you ought to leave. After all, we're all players, aren't we?'

The United players were delighted. When visiting the ground to watch Albion they had all seen the doorway marked PLAYERS AND OFFICIALS ONLY beside the main entrance. None of them had imagined he would walk through the doorway—at least, not until he was grown-up and had been signed as a professional by Albion. Each boy felt at least a couple of inches taller as he followed Dave Archer into the street.

As he bid them goodbye and wished them good luck in their next match he made a point of shaking each of them by the hand. Then, with a final wave, he strolled off into the night.

'I didn't know you knew Dave Archer

personally, Nick,' said Keith. He was just as impressed as he sounded. 'When did you meet him?'

'Oh, I've met him several times,' Nick replied with a casual air. 'I know a lot of the blokes at Albion. The club keeps an eye on promising young players, you know. That's why they come to watch me quite regularly. I expect one of their scouts will be turning up to see me play for United quite soon.'

'Oh,' said Keith quietly. None of the other boys said a word. But they were thinking a lot of things.

Five

Rain was hammering down as the United players jumped off a bus in Silversmith's Lane and headed across the fields to the ground where Clayton's Villa played their home matches. The Villa team had been got together by a boy called Frankie Clayton who lived in a very big house just off Silversmith's Lane. His father was a keen sportsman and a supporter of Aston Villa. So, as Frankie had called the first meeting of his team at his home, he decided that they should be known as Clayton's Villa.

Frankie's father actually owned a football pitch and changing-rooms equipped with hot-water showers. Clayton's Villa were never short of opponents willing to play away matches and Keith was very glad that Frankie's team were in the Sunday League. It was a pleasure to be able to use real changing-rooms where players could have a hot shower after the game. Normally United had to strip on the Common and it was only when they returned home that they could clean up properly (often that was the first thing they were *ordered* to do by parents appalled by the state their sons got into during one friendly soccer game).

'The pitch'll be a mud-bath today,' Nick remarked as they approached the ground. 'It'll really test our stamina. So it's a good job we had a real training session at Albion's ground.'

'Yes,' Keith agreed. 'I must say, your pal Mark Hedgemead looks pretty fit. And he's big, isn't he?'

'Big *and* fast,' Nick emphasized. 'That's how a full-back should be. He likes to join up in attacks so he should give us a bit of support up front. But he's quick in recovery as well. Just the sort of player your defence needs.'

Keith didn't like that reference to 'his' defence but he made no objection. He was glad enough that Nick had so quickly found a replacement for Simon Hallett. Although Simon himself claimed that his knee was better his mother had refused to pass him fit to play for United so soon after his injury. She had confirmed her decision that morning when it was already raining hard. Nick insisted that was the real reason she wouldn't allow Simon to play.

Frankie Clayton greeted the United team in front of the changing-rooms and, like a millionaire receiving guests for the weekend, told them to 'make yourselves at home'. As soon as they were out on the pitch, however, his welcome faded. The Villa were a hard, bustling side and it didn't bother them if their opponents collected a few bruises during the match. Those hot showers would soon ease the pain away, anyway.

Like Kevin Ripley, Frankie believed in giving his forward line all the fire-power he could muster. He himself played at centre-forward (it was *his* team, wasn't it?, as he was fond of telling people) between two strong and skilful ball-players. He hadn't shown the same keenness in recruiting defenders and both full-backs were on the small side. It didn't take Nick long to spot that weakness.

Gary Ansell was the first United player to have a chance of putting over a high centre. Both Nick and Kevin out-jumped the Villa full-backs but none of them actually got his head to the ball. The goalie, who was not short of inches, came off his line quickly to punch the ball away.

A few moments later Nick was having a word with some of his team-mates. He told Johnny Butler to drop back into a midfield position so that Harvey Slater could move up into the forward line. 'You won't find it easy to lift the ball in all this mud,' he told Johnny. 'Kevin's stronger than you so I'm moving him out on to the left-wing. You look after things in the middle, okay?' Johnny nodded and trotted off to take up his new position.

Next minute Nick gave fresh instructions to Mark Hedgemead and Edward Lancaster. He wanted them to switch positions so that Mark could add his height to the forward line. Edward, of course, fell in with the plan immediately. He would agree to do anything Nick asked—even to playing in goal if that was what Nick wanted.

Then it was Gary Ansell's turn. 'I want you to drop back a bit, Gary. I can pin-point my centres better than you so I'll go out on the wing more often.'

For once Nick had picked the wrong person to give orders to on the field. 'You must be joking,' Gary told him angrily. 'I'm a natural winger. So I'm staying out here. And, anyway, Keith's the captain, not you. I don't take orders from you, Smithy.'

Nick scowled. He hated being called 'Smithy', by anyone. But this wasn't the time to start a row. 'Look,' he replied sharply, 'I'm telling you what's best for the team. If somebody has a bright idea like this one then the team should use it. We're not playing for Keith—we're playing for United.'

He turned away before Gary could make a further protest. Ten minutes later United had the ball in the net and Gary was in no position to argue about how it had been done. He himself had lost the ball in a touch-line tackle. Nick, however, was on hand to win it back again and he shot off down the wing. He beat off a couple of defenders and moved inside—but only for a yard or two. Then he craftily lobbed the ball into the middle.

By now Mark Hedgemead and Harvey Slater had taken up good positions near the penalty spot. When they jumped for the ball they rose high above the Villa full-backs. The goalie hadn't risked coming out so far. He was dithering on his line when Harvey nodded the ball down to his left. Kevin was ready to pounce like a cat on a mouse. Before the goalie could decide which way to dive Kevin had cracked the ball past him into the bottom of the net.

He whooped with delight and flung both arms in the air. His enjoyment in scoring was always worth watching. It was in complete contrast to the way Nick celebrated his goals. At this moment Nick was just nodding his satisfaction at the way in which his plan had worked.

As usual Keith was quick to congratulate those players involved in the goal. 'Good work, Harvey. But I thought you were supposed to be in midfield these days.'

'Nick wanted me to go up front to use my height. That's why Mark's alongside me. He's half-an-inch taller than me—Nick says.'

That was the first Keith knew of the changes that had been made. He decided he'd have to have a word with Nick at half-time. He was beginning to feel that Nick was running the team.

Clayton's Villa pressed hard for the equalizer. Frankie himself made a couple of dangerous runs down the middle of the field—and earned plenty of applause from his father who was watching the game from the touch-line. Mr Clayton had made up his mind that one day his son would play centre-forward for the other Villa—Aston.

In spite of his work up front Mark was quickly back in defence and it was his tackle that stopped Frankie's best effort. Mark was as clever as Nick had said he was; he didn't waste the ball. He sent it to Keith Nash to start the best move of the whole match.

Keith passed to Gary who made progress before parting with it to Kevin. From Kevin it went to the eager Johnny Butler; he was just about to turn it inside to Nick when the Villa centre-half crashed into him. Johnny went sprawling and the referee blew for a foul. He had some stern words to say to the offender while Johnny picked himself up and wiped the mud off his face. Frankie came up to protest that it had only *looked* like a foul because Johnny was such a midget. The ref waved him away without even looking at him.

Nick took the kick. He knew exactly where

the ball should go and his aim was perfect. As the ball dropped Harvey Slater moved a foot to his right, jumped—and deflected the ball into the net off the upright.

He was thrilled at scoring a goal again. All his old confidence had come flooding back since he'd returned to the forward line. He rushed over to Nick. 'Great, just great!' he shouted, thumping Nick on the back. All he got in return was a faint grin. Nick was already thinking about the next goal.

In fact, that was the end of the scoring before half-time. All the players were glad to get out of the rain for a few minutes and into the luxury of the changing-rooms. Mr Clayton went off with Frankie, no doubt to talk about new tactics for the second half. In the United dressing-room the air soon became heated. The flare-up came as a result of a remark by Gary Ansell.

'That was a good goal of yours, Harvey—for a half-back, anyway,' he said loudly.

'Nick wanted me in the forward line for this match,' Harvey replied innocently. 'You see—'

'Oh, did he?' Gary went on, his eyebrows lifting. 'I hadn't heard United had a new captain

—and manager—and Prime Minister—and—'

'Hey, watch it, Ansell,' said Kevin, moving towards him threateningly. 'You trying to start something? Because if you are—'

'All right, lads, cool it!' Keith snapped. Kevin dropped his fists in surprise. He'd never heard Keith use that tone of voice before. Before Nick joined the team Kevin and Keith had been very close friends; Keith had often told him he didn't believe in shouting at people. Now, however, Keith seemed quite aggressive.

'We're all pals here and I don't want any trouble,' Keith announced. 'But there's only one captain and that's me. If we need to make changes I'll make 'em. Nobody else can do that. I give the orders around here, so remember that.'

'You do surprise me,' Nick said quietly. 'I didn't think you knew how to—give orders, I mean.'

Keith gritted his teeth. 'The same goes for you, Nick. Just because you're a good player you don't have the right to run the team. That's my job.'

'You were making a rotten mess of it till Nick came along,' Kevin shouted at him. 'Nick's forgotten more about football tactics than you'll ever know! He set up both goals this afternoon —you want to remember that.'

The row might have become even fiercer if there'd been time for it to develop. But at that moment the referee looked in and announced that he was ready to start the second half. He sensed there was trouble in the United team and grinned. 'If you lads get angry when you're winning goodness knows what you'd do if you were losing. So, come on, settle down. Football's only a game, you know. You should enjoy it.'

The rain was still trying to turn the pitch into a reservoir and perhaps it helped to wash away some of the anger that had gripped Keith and Gary and one or two of the others. Nick seemed quite unaffected by the arguments in the changing-room. His play was as brilliant as ever. Clayton's Villa tried every way they knew to stop him but Nick seemed to drift away from tackles.

Then, near the end of the match, one of the full-backs caught up with him. Nick was cutting in along the by-line when the defender tripped him on the edge of the 18-yard box. Immediately Nick took the free-kick himself. He blasted the ball away from the goal-mouth to the front of the penalty area. Johnny Butler, who had begun to run in on Nick's signal, took the ball on his right foot and drove it hard back towards the goal-mouth.

Once again, Kevin Ripley was in the right place at the right time. When the ball reached him he killed it instantly with his left instep. Although he had his back to the goal he didn't attempt to turn round. Instead he simply back-heeled the ball into the net.

It was exactly the sort of goal that Nick himself would have scored in the same circumstances. For once his face lit up and he hurried across to Kevin to put his arm round his shoulders. Keith, still irritated by the way Nick and Kevin were dominating the team, didn't say a word. Gary turned his head away and walked off. He still hadn't forgiven Nick for re-organizing the forward line.

When the whistle shrilled for the end of the match Frankie Clayton walked off the field with Nick. 'You've got a good team here, Nick,' he said, shaking hands with him. 'I'm glad we're not playing you every week.'

'Not bad,' Nick agreed. 'But we could still do

with some improvements here and there. We're not solid enough at the back sometimes.

'Oh, I don't know. Your defence seemed okay to me,' remarked Frankie. He couldn't say much else: the United defenders had prevented him from scoring.

Frankie had a loud voice and his conversation with Nick had carried to the rest of the United players. As soon as they were all in the dressing-room on their own Keith marched up to Nick and asked him what he meant by criticizing the defence. For some moments Nick just ignored him. He was busy removing his boots and socks and stripping off his shirt and shorts. Someone had already turned the showers on and he was going to make the most of the hot water. 'Work it out for yourself—if you can,' he said over his shoulder—and stepped under the nearest shower.

Only the fact that he was still wearing his playing kit stopped Keith from seizing Nick by the shoulder and demanding an apology. It seemed to him that Nick was not only trying to take over control of the team but insulting him by saying that he (Keith) didn't know much about football anyway.

Normally Kevin Ripley didn't bother removing any mud he'd collected during a match until hours later. Now, however, he was following Nick's example and was eager to take a shower. Deliberately he bumped into Keith as he passed him—and Keith staggered into the spray.

'Look at you,' Kevin sneered. 'You can't even stand up to a simple body charge. So don't try and argue with my pal. He's a genius.'

With Kevin and Nick both under the showers Keith was helpless because he didn't want to get his things wet; and by the time he'd stripped off his immediate anger might have cooled. Nick's next remark, however, caused United's captain to splutter as fiercely as the shower sprinklers.

'Kevin's right,' Nick said, nodding slowly with a solemn face to show that he meant it. 'I think it's time you paid me to play for United. Dozens of other teams want me to play for them. So if you want to keep me you'll have to pay me. I'm worth it because I make sure you win your matches.'

Gary was flabbergasted. But, unlike Keith, he hadn't lost his voice. 'Get lost! You must be nuts, Smithy! I think we were crazy to pay money

for your transfer. We'd be even stupider to give you money to play for United.'

'Well, if I don't get paid I'm not playing any more for you,' Nick replied calmly. He was working up a good lather on his arms and obviously enjoying every moment of his shower. 'Without me—and Kevin—United would be no good at all. If I played *against* you I'd score a dozen goals before half-time.'

'If Nick goes, I go as well,' Kevin added, coming in on cue. But he didn't make the mistake of suggesting that he also should be paid for playing for United.

'Don't forget I showed you lot how to get fit,' Nick went on. 'We won this match today because of the extra training we did. That's how we got fit. Or some of us did, anyway.'

'I got fit by doing weight-lifting,' Gary retorted. 'I've been training on my own. I can lift 60 lbs. in weights. Well, nearly 60 lbs. That's real fitness, Smithy.'

'Weight-lifting's only good for arms and shoulders,' Nick pointed out. 'It's strong leg muscles and stamina you want.'

'If you're so strong why don't you strip off

and show us your big muscles,' Kevin grinned. 'Come and have a shower with us—or are you scared you'll melt in the hot water? Come on, Ansell, I'll warm it up for you—if you can stand it.'

'If I got under the same shower as you two I wouldn't get clean—I'd get dirtier from using the same water.'

Kevin laughed. 'You just daren't show us your weedy body.'

Keith was in a quandary. The idea of paying money to one of the United team to play for them was terrible. Yet he had no doubt that Nick really meant what he'd said. And if Nick got paid then Kevin would be sure to demand payment as well. Those two were now as thick as thieves; and thieves were what they were because they were trying to rob United.

On the other hand, United couldn't afford to lose them. The team had been having a bad time before Nick joined them. Without Nick and Kevin it would probably be difficult to field a full team. United's hopes of winning the League title would disappear like a mouse down a hole.

The whole business made him feel quite sick.

He didn't like rows at the best of times; the bitterness of this afternoon horrified him. United meant everything to him: it was *his* team and he wasn't going to allow it to break up. Somehow he'd just have to find a solution to his problems.

Keith was almost dressed by the time Nick came out from under the showers. Even with the water dripping off him United's star forward looked as cool and composed as ever.

'Look,' Keith said to him quietly, 'we'll have to talk things over. We've got to work things out between us. We'll have a meeting after our training session on Thursday night. I'll have sorted something out by then.'

'You'd better,' Nick replied. 'Otherwise I'll probably be playing for another team next Sunday.'

Six

The roar of the engines was deafening. Gary Ansell, standing on the edge of the track, had to move back hurriedly as one motor-cycle skidded past him. It sent up a spray of mud which Gary only just avoided. He thought the machine was out of control; but the rider, a boy of his own age, soon straightened it out and went off in pursuit of the other bikes.

Gary looked down the track, waiting for Kevin Ripley to appear on his blue and white Kawasaki motor-bike. He'd expected Kevin to be among the leaders, even though this was only a practice scramble. Perhaps he'd been having trouble on one of the bends. Kevin had admitted he was new to this game and still had a lot to learn. That wasn't Kevin's usual attitude in anything but perhaps he was changing a bit.

Certainly Gary had been very surprised when Kevin had called at his home the previous evening, a Friday. It was less than twenty-four hours after United's training session following the match with Clayton's Villa. All the members of the team had turned up but none of them enjoyed it very much. The rows that had broken out on the Sunday were soon in full swing again.

Keith's anger had been simmering for four days and it came to the boil when Nick arrived and wanted to change the training methods. Keith, a fitness fanatic at times, was organizing press-ups and short, sharp sprints. Nick said they should have some dribbling practice between obstacles. Reasonably enough, Keith pointed out that that would only be of benefit to the forwards; and then reminded Nick that he gave the orders because he was captain.

Within moments everyone seemed to be quarrelling with everyone else until Nick and Kevin said they were going. Keith, shaken by the fierceness of the arguments, called after them to ask if they were going to play for United on Sunday. Nick didn't bother to answer and Kevin yelled back: 'Not a chance! We don't play with idiots.'

Keith was prepared to rush after them to try and smooth things over but Gary had held him back. 'Let 'em go, Keith. If they don't want us, we don't want them.' Keith hesitated—and the chance of repairing the damage that night was lost. When the rest of the team went home soon afterwards nobody had any idea of what was going to happen on Sunday.

The following evening Gary had been wrestling with a tricky maths problem in his homework when Kevin called. They attended the same school and played in the same team but they had never been particularly pally; each tended to think of the other as a rival. Now, however, Kevin was in a very friendly mood.

He had come with an invitation: he wanted Gary to go with him to a motor-cycle scramble next morning. It wasn't, he pointed out, a meeting for grown-ups: it was for schoolboys and he himself would be one of the riders. His father had bought him a motor-bike a few weeks ago and Kevin couldn't resist adding that he was pretty good at the sport already.

Gary was more than interested; he'd watched a lot of scrambling on television and wished he could do it one day. He hadn't imagined that boys of his age were allowed to ride motor-bikes; in any case, they'd be too heavy for a boy to handle. Oh, these were smaller bikes, Kevin said—but still pretty powerful. One boy actually had a Yamaha, a 97 c.c. model. All the riders were members of the Junior Motor-Cycle Federation which they could join from the age of eight upwards. England and Sweden were the only countries that allowed boys to ride motor-cycles for scrambling. Naturally Kevin, the boy who was determined to be a bank manager, knew all the details.

Gary hadn't needed much persuading, especially as Kevin had hinted that he might be allowed to have a ride later in the morning. He guessed that Kevin might have a reason for inviting him but as he didn't mention it that evening Gary didn't ask.

Now that he was actually at Rawstone Edge, the hilly circuit where the meeting was taking place, he'd forgotten about the motive for the invitation. He was enjoying the sight of the bikes and the riders in action and the smell of the burning oil and petrol fumes.

Next minute Kevin came bouncing along the muddy track. Even with his distinctive orange crash helmet and black goggles to keep the dirt out of his eyes he was not easy to recognize. He appeared to have been in a mud-bath already. But his engine was roaring excitingly and he was getting up a good speed ('We sometimes go as fast as 40 m.p.h. on the straight,' he told Gary).

Of course, it wouldn't have been the real Kevin if he hadn't tried to show-off. As he drew level with Gary he stood up in the foot-rests. The bike wobbled dangerously at that moment and Kevin hastily sat down again. Gary had thought the bike was going to fall over but somehow Kevin kept it balanced. His confidence soon returned and he waved a hand as he disappeared round a bend.

As this was only a practice run Gary didn't expect his friend to return along this route so he set off to walk to the starting point. There was going to be a race later on and it was after that he hoped to get a ride. Kevin had admitted that he didn't know much about engines but one of the mechanics who always attended the scrambles

was going to teach him how to strip and clean and repair his bike.

Most of the riders had assembled at the starting point when Gary arrived. He saw that some of the boys were younger than himself and he felt very envious about their luck in being able to compete in scrambles. He supposed a bike cost a lot of money and he doubted that his father could afford one. All the same, if he started saving his own money his father might be willing to help later on. Perhaps he could drop a few hints when his father was in a good mood ... after he'd won at golf, for instance.

Gary was already racing ahead—in his thoughts, anyway—to the day when he might be competing in the T.T. races in the Isle of Man when he heard an engine note different from the rest. It sounded as if the engine was coughing. Moments later Kevin came into sight. It was obvious that there was something wrong with his machine.

A man in overalls went over to him as Kevin came to a stop. 'Must be something wrong with the fuel system,' Kevin remarked knowledgeably as Gary came up. Kevin pushed his goggles up and watched as the mechanic went to work with a spanner.

'It's been acting up all morning,' Kevin said. 'But I'm going to take part in this even if it kills me.'

The mechanic stood up. 'Just take it easy on the first circuit,' he advised. 'I think I know what the trouble is but we might have to strip it right down later. So don't go mad, son.'

Kevin just nodded. He had a rather superior air which Gary decided was for his benefit. 'We'll be off in a minute,' he said to Gary. 'Go up to the top of the hill over there. You'll see me come up like a rocket. We just fly over the top—absolutely airborne. It's great. That's the best place on the whole circuit.

By now the mechanic had moved away and Gary wondered what he would have said if he'd heard Kevin's words. Gary didn't say anything because he could see that the riders were lining up and he didn't want to miss the hill climb. Kevin's engine seemed to be all right again judging by the rhythmic noise it was making.

Gary just had time to reach the summit of the steep bank by using a short cut before the starting signal was given. The riders surged away in a bunch and Kevin's orange helmet was easily visible in the middle of them.

They all approached the hill at a very fast speed. Kevin was not riding to his mechanic's instructions because he'd already forced his way into the leading group. He was in third place, only a yard or so behind the pacesetters, as they charged up the hill. Gary thought they were all showing a lot of courage to ride at such a speed.

The first bike really did take off as it soared over the summit. It was a thrilling sight and Gary turned to watch the bike touch down again on the descent. He'd taken his eye off Kevin and so he missed exactly what happened. Next moment, however, he had to leap for safety as a bike hurtled towards him on its side. There was a lot of shouting mingled with the roar of engines. When the bike came to rest with a shuddering crash against a grassy hillock Kevin was underneath it. The machine was pinning him to the ground.

Gary dashed over to the scene of the accident. He was not the only spectator at that point but he reached Kevin first. The remainder of the riders shot past over the top of the hill; it seemed to Gary that they missed him only by inches.

He lifted the motor-cycle off Kevin and was surprised how light it was. The front wheel, with its ribbed tyre, was still spinning round. But the engine was silent.

'Kevin! Are you all right?' he asked anxiously. Kevin's eyes were closed and Gary was frightened. Then, to his immense relief, Kevin opened his eyes. For a moment he looked dazed, staring at Gary without apparently seeing him. Then, gently, he shook his head and the light came back into his eyes.

'That rotten engine!' he exploded suddenly. 'It cut out on me. Then somebody bashed into my back tyre and knocked me over. I could've been killed!'

Kevin's friend, the mechanic, had now arrived. The first thing he did was to examine the bike. Then he turned to Kevin.

'You young fool,' he said, quite quietly. 'I told you to take it easy. You're lucky you weren't hurt. Look, when I tell you a thing I mean it. You went off like a jet plane down a runway. Fortunately, the bike's not badly damaged. But you won't be riding it again for a week or two.'

That silenced Kevin. Gary, too, was dismayed. He knew now that he wouldn't be having a ride that morning. He'd been looking forward to his turn all morning. Now it would be a fortnight at least before he could have his first ride on a motor-bike built for scrambling.

Kevin had got to his feet but after one stumbling step he sat down again. There was pain on his face as he started to rub his knee. Gary didn't feel very sympathetic but he inquired what was wrong.

'I must have twisted it when the bike fell over. It hurts a lot.'

Usually Kevin shrugged off any injuries at soccer so Gary knew his friend really must be in pain. His thoughts flashed ahead to United's game the next day.

Before Gary could say anything Kevin's father came up. Kevin told him what had happened and Mr Ripley had a look at his knee.

'A severe sprain, I should think,' he pronounced. 'You'll have to rest it up for a few days. Come on, I'll take you home. Your mother will know how to make it easier for you.' He told Kevin to hang on while he fetched the car; he didn't seem to mind the idea of driving it over all the rough ground to the foot of the hill.

'So you won't be able to play tomorrow,' Gary said, sitting down beside Kevin.

''Fraid not. You'll be in a bad way without me —and Nick.'

'Has Nick definitely told you he's not going to play?'

'Well, that was what I was going to talk to you

about after the scramble, Gary. You see, Nick and I think Keith's no good as captain. He has no new ideas and he doesn't really *lead* the team. He's too soft. He won't tell players when they do things wrong. I think Nick should be captain—and he agrees. I mean, he'll take on the job if the rest of the team want him.'

'But Keith won't give up the captaincy. It's *his* team.'

'Maybe it used to be. But it isn't any more. Nick's re-organized it—and he can find new players, like Mark Hedgemead. So he should lead it. Keith's pig-headed, he won't listen to us. But you're his best pal. If you told him that *you* wanted Nick to be captain we reckon Keith would have to agree. The rest of the team would vote for Nick, anyway.'

'But what if Keith won't agree? I mean, I can't *make* him—even if I wanted to.'

'Then United's finished. We'll all pull out and form a new team, under Nick and me. Look, Gary, we don't want to do that—but we will if Keith won't give in.'

The sound of the car bouncing over the turf and the rutted track grew louder. In a moment or two Mr Ripley would be coming to fetch Kevin. Their conversation would be over. Kevin had the last word.

'Gary, you've got to go and tell Keith all this. You've *got* to make him see things our way. If you don't, it's the end for United.'

Seven

Gary trudged along the road to Keith's home, head down and deep in thought. He could imagine what Keith's reaction would be to the news that Gary had for him. He didn't think Keith would agree to give up the captaincy. After all, United was his team: he had brought the players together, arranged the fixtures and got them into the Sunday Junior League.

On the other hand, without Nick and Kevin the team wouldn't be much of a force in the League. They were the chief goal-scorers and they had built up a fine partnership. Worse still, it was probably true, as Kevin had said, that most members of the team would vote for Nick as captain—and if Nick didn't get the job they would go off with him to form a new team. Apart from Kevin himself, the ones who would be on Nick's side in any argument were Edward Lancaster, Harvey Slater, Johnny Butler, Mark Hedgemead and possibly Alex Hornsey. They were more than enough to give Nick a clear majority in a vote.

Gary couldn't decide what advice he should give to Keith. He wanted to be loyal to his friend; but, equally, he didn't want to see the break-up of United. It really was a terrible problem. He wished there was someone he could turn to for help. But there wasn't anyone. They—Keith and himself—would have to find a solution on their own.

When he rang the bell at Keith's home it was Mrs Nash who came to the door. Keith, she said, had gone to the shop to fetch her some groceries but Gary was welcome to come in and wait for him. She seemed pleased to see him and offered him a glass of lemonade. Gary liked her very much: she seemed a lot younger than most mothers and was very pretty. Most important of all, in Gary's view, she took a great interest in Keith's football team.

'I must say, Gary,' she said chattily while he was sipping his lemonade in the kitchen, 'you

104

look a bit miserable. Just like Keith. He's been down in the dumps all week. He won't tell me what's wrong but I have my suspicions.

'It's about the football team, isn't it? I thought you were such a happy team. You've been winning your matches, haven't you? I know that because I always ask Keith the result when he comes in. So tell me your troubles.'

Gary hesitated. He didn't want to say too much. If Keith felt unable to tell his mother what was going on then it would be disloyal of Gary to reveal their troubles. Yet surely Mrs Nash would be on Keith's side. Moreover, Gary didn't want to be impolite by refusing to discuss the team.

'Well, you see, Mrs Nash,' he said slowly, taking another sip of lemonade between every word, 'one of the boys wants to take over as captain from Keith. He thinks he's the best player in the side and so he should run the team.'

'And is he?—the best player in the side, I mean.'

'Ye-es, I suppose so,' Gary had to admit. 'He's very clever and he scores goals. He says that Albion are watching him for the future. So they must think he's good, too.'

'No wonder Keith's worried. Poor Keith. He takes his job as captain so seriously. What's this other boy's name?'

'Nick Abel-Smith.'

'Oh, that one. I know his mother. Isn't he the one you paid a transfer fee for or something like that? I thought that was rather amusing.'

'Yes, we did!' Gary replied hotly. 'And a rotten deal it's turned out. He even wants paying for playing now.'

'What! Why that's outrageous.' Mrs Nash looked very shocked. 'You boys are becoming just as bad as the men, the professional footballers. They're always wanting more money. I think they get quite enough as it is.

'But Gary, he can't be serious! I mean, you're only schoolboys. You've only got your pocket money.'

'Oh, he means it all right, Mrs Nash. He says if we don't pay him he'll go to another team.'

'Well, that's outrageous,' Mrs Nash repeated. 'I shall speak to his mother about it. I don't suppose she'll approve of such goings-on.'

While she was saying that the door had opened and Keith stepped into the kitchen. He looked very angry as he dumped a bag of groceries on the table.

'Who are you talking about?' he demanded to know. 'Is this something to do with United?'

'Gary's been telling me about this boy Nick Abel-Smith,' his mother said. 'Apparently he wants to be paid for playing for your team. I think that's quite wicked. So I'm going to have a quiet word with his mother about it. He'll soon change his tune when she hears about it.'

'You shouldn't have said anything,' Keith muttered to Gary between clenched teeth. 'Coming here and blabbing about United. That's private.'

'Now don't take that attitude, Keith,' Mrs Nash said sharply. 'Gary is a very loyal friend of yours. He was quite right to tell me, your mother, about what's going on. I guessed you weren't happy with your football games recently. Now I know why. I've a good mind to go round and see Shirley Abel-Smith this minute.'

'No, please don't do that,' Keith said hurriedly. 'We can sort it out ourselves.'

'But how, Keith?' Gary asked. 'I came to tell you what's happened. Kevin's injured his leg, falling off a motor-bike, so he can't play tomorrow. And he told me that Nick wants to take over as captain. If you won't let him be captain he'll get the rest of the players to go off with him and form a new team. He says United will be finished then.'

'Where did Kevin tell you all this? At your house?'

'Well, not really.' Gary was feeling a bit embarrassed. 'Actually, I went to a motor-cycle scramble with him. He's got his own bike there. It was this morning. That was when he told me—after he was injured.'

'Oh, I see. So you're on his side now, are you? Well thanks very much, Ansell. I like to know who my enemies are.'

'Keith, you can stop that at once!' Mrs Nash said. 'Gary's your friend, that should be obvious to you. He wouldn't be here otherwise, would he? It's plain he's just as worried about things as you are. Gary, you want Keith to stay as captain of United, don't you?'

'Oh, yes, Mrs Nash, of course I do.' Gary was very thankful she understood how he felt. 'I came to tell Keith the news and ask what he was going to do. I'm on his side. Really I am, Keith. Honest.'

'All right—sorry,' Keith said. 'But I've been thinking about things. I decided that as I'm captain I have to decide things for myself. And I know how to deal with Nick Abel-Smith. I know how to fix him, all right.'

'How?' Gary asked eagerly. Mrs Nash appeared just as interested to hear Keith's plans as well.

'I'm going to write to Dave Archer. I'm going to tell him that Nick's demanding money to play for an amateur team. Dave will know that's all wrong. So Dave will tell Albion's scout—the one who's supposed to be keeping an eye on Nick. And the scout will tell Nick to forget it, otherwise Albion will have nothing more to do with him.

'If Nick tries to join another team Albion will tell them what he's up to. Anyway, Nick will have to do what Albion tells him because he's mad keen to play for them when he's older.'

'Hey, that's a brilliant idea,' Gary said delightedly. And Mrs Nash nodded her approval. She was pleased that her son had found a way of solving his own problems.

'I've also been doing a bit of scouting of my

own,' Keith went on. 'This morning, while you were being pally with that traitor Kevin, I went to see a couple of boys who used to play for Longton Rangers. Their team dropped out of the League, you know. Well, they haven't got fixed up with anyone else so they're keen to play for United. They can turn out for us tomorrow, if we need them.'

'Oh, that's great,' Gary said. He'd always liked Keith; now he admired the way he had set about dealing with the troubles that were affecting United. 'What positions do they play, Keith?'

'Rex Colmer's a striker. He's tall and can head the ball. So that's useful. Larry Underwood is a half-back. Underwood's not as good as Colmer but I think he'll be okay. Anyway, we need some reserves.'

'We'll have to play one of them tomorrow because Kevin's definitely out.'

'Okay, so Colmer comes in. And if Abel-Smith causes any trouble I'll replace him with Underwood who can be the substitute.'

'What if Smithy tries to take over as captain, though?'

'I'll just tell him to push off. I'll tell him that

if he mentions money again I'll write to Dave Archer about him. That'll fix Nick Abel-Smith.

'I'm captain of United because I know how to fix things. I don't shout at players all the time like Kevin would—and I don't push them around like Smithy does. But the team have confidence in me.'

'Well said, Keith,' his mother smiled. 'I think you've just earned yourself a super lunch today. Would you like to have your lunch with us, Gary? I'm sure you and Keith want to talk over tactics for the next match, don't you?'

'Oh yes, please.' Gary was delighted. 'Thank you very much, Mrs Nash.'

Within a very short time she'd produced a feast of eggs and beans and chips and home-made apple pie. It was a meal they all enjoyed together; every mouthful of it.

When the United players assembled on the Common the following afternoon for their League match with Green Park Juniors Nick Abel-Smith was not among them.

Keith admitted privately to Gary that the absence of Nick and Kevin was a blow to the team. He wondered how United would manage without their two leading goalscorers. Although he now disliked Nick he had a great respect for his talents as a footballer.

All the same, it was Keith's belief that the team was greater than any individual player. He was about to say so to Gary when he spotted Nick strolling across the Common. Nick was coming in their direction but he didn't seem to be in any hurry. Keith had been on the point of asking Harvey Slater to take over as centre-forward and re-placing him in midfield with Larry Underwood. Now he waited to see what Nick had to say.

'Sorry I'm a bit late,' Nick said. 'I dropped in to see how Kevin is. Nobody else from United had bothered to go and see him.'

Keith felt a bit guilty about that; but he'd been so busy he hadn't had time. 'Are you playing for us today?' he asked Nick. 'But we're not going to pay you any money if you do play. That's out.'

'I didn't think you would. Still, I'll play today. You're going to need me. I don't know what sort of service I'm going to get without Kevin in the side.'

'Oh, we'll see you get the ball,' Keith told him. 'There are ten other players in the team, you know.'

Green Park were not one of the most powerful sides in the League and Keith was hoping for a good victory to boost United's chances of the championship. Unhappily, United didn't make a very good start.

Keith himself slipped when going in for a tackle on Park's left-winger, a boy called Appleby who was almost as fast as Gary Ansell. Appleby put over a good cross. Mark Hedgemead should have cleared it but he missed his kick completely. Then Alex Hornsey made United's third mistake —and that cost them a goal.

For when Park's inside-right fastened on to the loose ball and tried a shot at goal Alex made a hash of his save. The ball went into his arms and straight out again. The inside-right, hardly able to believe his luck, rushed in and with the toe of his boot he pushed the ball into the net.

Keith, annoyed with himself for his own mistake, didn't say anything. But he wasn't pleased to see Nick shaking his head sadly as if to say 'That rotten defence again . . .' He felt that Nick should be thinking about how to score the equalizer.

That early goal seemed to inspire Green Park. Their defence joined in the next attack. United were under a lot of pressure for a long spell but at last Harvey got the ball away to his forwards. Rex Colmer quickly showed that he knew what he was doing when he supplied Nick with an excellent pass.

Park's defence was now wide open. Nick took the ball down the middle, easily beat the one defender who was left to tackle him and so had only the goalie to beat. Nick didn't miss chances like that. Cool as ever he allowed the goalkeeper to dive at the ball, pulled it away from those clutching hands and then very gently stroked it into the net.

His team-mates were loud in their praise as usual but Nick took no notice of them. The next time the ball came to him he did a lot of fancy dribbling across the field and then tried a shot on the turn that hit the cross-bar. He was showing Green Park—and his own players—just how good he was.

So nobody was surprised that it was Nick who

scored the goal that gave United the lead. Gary won a free-kick just outside the penalty area a couple of minutes before half-time. He took it himself and lifted the ball into the goal-mouth. A Park defender tried to head it away but it didn't go very far. Harvey Slater nodded it forward again. Nick, jumping higher than anyone else, had his back to the goal—and his clever back-header took everyone completely by surprise.

United held on to their advantage until three minutes from the end. Appleby was still Park's best raider and when he got the ball in the middle of the field he went straight for goal. Larry Underwood, who'd come on in place of Mark, who had had a nasty bang on his knee, made a very feeble attempt at a tackle. The Park winger went round him and then tried a long-range shot. Hornsey was well off his goal-line—and the ball sailed over his head to drop into the net.

That equalizer cost United a point. Keith was quite furious about it. Nick merely looked annoyed. As the teams left the field he spoke to Keith.

'Well, that's the last game I'm playing for you lot,' he announced. 'I score goals to win matches.

I don't want to play for a team that just gives 'em away at the other end. United aren't good enough for me.'

'But we've got an important Cup-tie next week,' Keith reminded him.

'Hard luck. I reckon you've no chance at all with that defence—and without me.'

Eight

Kevin Ripley was still not fully fit after his injury but that wasn't going to keep him out of United's team if he could help it. Nick had paid him a visit at his home on Wednesday evening and since then he'd trained hard every minute he could spare. Although Keith and Gary hadn't said much to him Kevin knew United needed him. Their Cup opponents, St Joseph's Church, were a very strong side.

Nick had called to say that he had joined another team. He said they had plenty of good players so there wasn't a place for Kevin. Nick hadn't mentioned money so Kevin guessed his friend had given up the idea of asking for payment for playing.

In a way, Kevin wasn't sorry Nick was leaving United. He suspected that most of the players didn't really like him. Most of the time he played only for himself, not for the team. That was what Keith had said and Kevin now agreed with his captain, especially as Nick obviously hadn't bothered to find him a place in his new team. Nick had left without scoring ten goals for United so Kevin shared out the remaining 50p of the transfer money among the team and tried to forget the whole episode.

On Sunday afternoon it was just like old times to go off to the Common in company with Keith and Gary. On the way they talked about tactics and how the match might be played. Keith said that he wanted to keep Harvey Slater at centre-forward with Rex Colmer alongside him as co-striker. He suggested that Kevin might try to play more in midfield. Gary said he thought that was a good idea.

Kevin was about to protest that he was a natural goal-scorer and so he would be wasted in midfield. He stopped himself just in time.

For he realized that probably they were testing him. If United really meant everything to him he should be prepared to play anywhere for them. In any case, a good footballer could play in any position. So Kevin merely said: 'Okay, if that's what you want. I'll push the ball through.' But he added: 'Mind you, if we get on top I'll be going through for a shot myself when the chance comes.'

One by one the rest of the players arrived and Keith was relieved to see that Mark Hedgemead was among them. He was glad that Mark was staying loyal to United and not following his friend Abel-Smith to another team.

The St Joseph's players wore a dazzling all-gold strip. They had brought a coach-load of supporters with them. When the teams took the field those fans began to sing very heartily. Their favourite number, of course, was 'And when the Saints go marching in...'

Keith had a final word for his team. 'This is a big one. Give all you've got for United. If we can win the Cup as well as the League everybody'll have to admit we're the best team in England. So come on, lads, we can do it.'

St Joseph's started as if they, too, believed they could do the Double. United kicked off with Harvey slipping the ball sideways to Rex Colmer —but that was as far as the ball went. For Rex hesitated and the St Joseph's inside-right charged at him like a bull. Rex was knocked to the ground and he didn't get up. The referee's whistle blew and the players crowded round the injured boy.

While a man came on to the field to attend to Rex the referee gave a very stern warning to St Joseph's inside-right, Robin Wolfe. The offender protested that it was a fair charge but the referee didn't agree. He awarded United a free-kick. First, however, Rex had to be helped off the field. His eyes were open now but he looked very dazed. Keith thought about bringing on his substitute, Larry Underwood, right away but decided to wait to see if Rex recovered. It was a bad blow to lose a player who hadn't even had time to kick a ball in the match before he was injured.

The United players took some time to settle down after that incident and St Joseph's began to swing the ball around with a lot of confidence. They had been beaten in the Cup Final the previous season and they were determined to win the trophy this time. Robin Wolfe was living up to his surname rather than his first name— chasing after the ball wherever it went and seizing every opening for a snap shot at goal.

Edward Lancaster was having a terrible time trying to mark him. So far United hadn't managed to set up a single attack.

Keith was keeping an eye on Rex Colmer who was on his feet but still receiving attention from St Joseph's trainer. Because he was thinking about the injury problem Keith's concentration on the game weakened for a few moments. And that was when St Joseph's scored.

Mark was rather slow to clear the ball on the edge of the penalty area. He tried to boot it away when challenged by the centre-forward but the ball struck his opponent's leg and flew across the penalty area.

Keith, still watching what was happening off the field, was caught out of position. The Saints' inside-left moved in behind him and knocked the ball back into the middle. Wolfe was in exactly the right place and he hooked the ball viciously into the net.

The first goal in a Cup-tie is always important; St Joseph's were elated, United dismayed. Keith, well aware of his own mistake, didn't condemn his players. 'Come on, lads,' he called, 'we can still beat this lot.'

The next blow, however, was hardest of all to take. Robin Wolfe's enthusiasm had increased as a result of scoring. Now, as a ball went out of play over the touch-line, he raced after it. Larry Underwood was stationed at that point and he moved to pick up the ball; he meant to give it to Keith because it was a throw-in for United. In his excitement Wolfe kept going, barged into Larry and sent him flying. His boot had caught United's substitute on the knee and Larry was in pain.

This time the referee took Wolfe's name and told him: 'One more trick like that from you, sonny, and I'll send you off for ungentlemanly conduct.' Robin apologized and the referee let him go back on to the field. Larry was not so lucky. His knee was already beginning to swell and there was no hope of his playing that afternoon. So now United had lost their substitute before he could even take part in the game.

Keith shook his head in disbelief at this double twist of fate. All he could hope now was that Rex would recover for the second half.

The game continued to be a hard one in every sense of the word. Fouls were being committed regularly, most of them by St Joseph's. Although many of their team were choir boys there was nothing angelic about their play. Perhaps this was because they had to behave in church on Sunday morning and Sunday evening and so they made the most of their freedom in the afternoon.

The referee, however, was aware of what was going on and after a bad foul on Mark he took the captain of St Joseph's on one side and told him to discipline his players—or else. He wasn't going to stand for any more trouble.

At half-time Keith felt rather relieved that United were only one goal down. Rex told him he was still feeling a bit dizzy but he'd play if he was needed. 'Sit down for a bit and I'll call you on later,' Keith said and then went to have a word with the rest of the team. 'We're still in with a chance lads, so keep trying,' he said. 'It's our turn for a bit of luck in the second half.'

As they returned to the field Edward Lancaster murmured to Gary: 'You know, Keith's a good skipper. He encourages his players. He doesn't boss them about and he keeps calm. All he thinks about is United. All Nick Abel-Smith thinks about is himself.'

Gary nodded his agreement. Even if United lost

he wouldn't regret the fact that Smithy was no longer in the team.

Both sides began the second half with the aim of attacking. United were determined to get an equalizer, St Joseph's were just as keen to increase their lead to a winning score.

After only five minutes United got the break they'd been hoping for—and they were back on level terms. Kevin had been doing a great deal of work in midfield. He still felt twinges of pain in his knee occasionally but he refused to let that bother him. Now, as an opponent slipped in front of him, he darted upfield with the ball.

A defender tried to block his route to goal but Kevin flicked the ball against the boy's legs, seized the rebound and went past him. That was a trick he'd learned from Nick. Almost as soon as he'd crossed the 18-yard line he fired in a hard shot. The goalie was late in diving, the ball clipped the base of the near upright—and entered the net. United had equalized.

Kevin took his success quite calmly—for him.. He merely jumped with delight and ran back to the centre-circle with his arm held high in triumph. Normally he'd have whooped and turned cart-wheels to celebrate such a goal in such a match. Perhaps he'd learned something else from Nick.

That goal was an inspiration to United. A few minutes later Rex Colmer made his own decision to return to the field of play. Keith motioned to him to stay in midfield while Kevin moved up into the attack. United had to go all out for the winner now. The team was tiring as a result of playing so long with only ten men. If St Joseph's went ahead again that would probably be the end of United.

St Joseph's had put just as much effort into the game. Some of the choir boys were almost on their knees—and they were praying for another goal for their side.

With just one minute to go to full-time those prayers were answered. St Joseph's won a corner on the right. Instead of trying to lift the ball into the middle the winger turned it back to a team-mate. He ran forward for a couple of yards before hitting a low shot into the crowded penalty area. Nobody could control it and there was a wild scramble.

Suddenly it bobbed up in front of Robin Wolfe.

He lashed at it with all his strength. The ball flew into the air, struck the referee on his shoulder and then, quite slowly, looped over the goalie's head and fell into the net.

'Sorry, lads,' the ref said to the United players. 'That's a bit of bad luck for you because the referee is just part of the fittings. I have to award a goal—just as if the ball had gone in off a post.'

That lucky goal won the Cup-tie for St Joseph's because there was no time for United to save the game. At the end of the match they were sad but, as Keith said, there was no need to be downhearted. They'd had a lot of bad luck but they'd played some great football.

'That's because we're a real team—we play for each other,' he added. 'We're united now for United.'